I0594287

Elusive Happiness

A Novel

Written & Illustrated

by

Joyce Lange Cowen

NENGE BOOKS, Australia

Elusive Happiness
By Joyce Lange Cowen

Layout and desktop by Nenge Books
Published by Nenge Books, Australia
ABN 26809396184
email: nengebooks1@gmail.com
www.nengebooks.com

ISBN 978-0-6488206-2-8

Also available as an ebook - ISBN 978-0-6488206-3-5

Dedicated to my family

God answers prayers, don't give up.
He always hears our requests when we pray.
Keep the faith as Margo has all through her
trials.

To Geoff, Julie and Ruth

You have always been a blessing to us,
thank you for caring for us in our old age
and the love you have shown to us.

Mum and Dad

Acknowledgements

I would like to acknowledge the invaluable assistance of my daughter Julie Cason, and my friend Dulcie Reeves for typing and assisting in preparation of the manuscript.

Joyce Lange Cowen

June 2020

Contents

Margo's Lifestyle

Cedric was nearly at the end of the homeward track when he saw Martin Fuller's rider-less horse. 'He must have been thrown off,' he thought. Cedric increased his pace, and then to his surprise, Martin stumbled towards him and then collapsed.

It was Margo Fuller's twenty second birthday - she and her mum, Eve, had prepared a picnic lunch and a special birthday cake they would enjoy after their ride out to the dam. They would eat well. As they set out, Martin, her father, had not yet finished his chores and said he would catch up later.

Cedric Carlyal, their neighbor's son, had joined them. Margo enjoyed going riding together with him often, aware of her feelings towards him. He had two more years of study at university to go, and Margo hoped Cedric would give her some indication of his feelings for her today.

They rode on - the horses ambling along at an enjoyable pace, Eve and Margo chatting amiably about the next phase in Margo's life and education, after having two gap years, that had stretched out to four gap years, helping her father on the property.

Margo now wanted to go to university. She hoped to work with computers – possibly enjoy secretarial work, and who knows might end up being a personal assistant to a politician. She loved politics; she and her dad often had

Margo

debates – her mum kept out of these, as she didn't care much for that political stuff.

Martin had not caught up and so, after an hour had passed, Cedric casually suggested that he would ride back and check. Inwardly he was concerned. He cantered off on his black gelding, a beautiful horse his dad had given him to ride when he came home on holidays from university.

When he found Martin, Cedric quickly dismounted and hurried to his side – the man was unconscious but alive. Cedric felt his pulse; Martin's heart beat rapidly. Cedric, who was studying to be a medical doctor, knew not to move him – Martin could have a broken spine or internal injuries.

As they rode back, Margo and Eve found the men and were distressed to see Martin on the ground unconscious. Cantering up to join Cedric, both quickly dismounted as he phoned for an ambulance. The women, holding back tears, stayed with Martin until an ambulance arrived. He was examined carefully at the local hospital then air lifted to Brisbane Base, the women accompanying him in the helicopter.

The doctors examined him and diagnosed excessive internal bleeding. His life now hung by a thread. The women prayed that if it was God's will Martin would recover, and if not, that he would not be in too much pain. Cedric wasted no time driving to the Base Hospital and joined the women there; all were advised to book into a motel close by where they could be contacted.

Early next morning they received the dreaded news by phone. Overcome with grief, they all wept tears of sadness, consoling each other. After regaining their composure they

went back to the hospital to see their beloved husband
and father, offering up a prayer of thanksgiving to God for
Martin's life. They were indeed thankful they had been a
part of the life of this wonderful man, who had been so
very dedicated to them. Cedric drove the women out to
the closest beach where they all could share their grief.
Perhaps the soothing of the waves would comfort them
all, he thought.

Martin's Funeral

Cedric's mother, Jane, came over to visit Eve and Margo to comfort them. She brought a casserole and inquired if there was anything else she could do, as the funeral was to take place tomorrow. Eve suggested Jane might like to arrange flowers in the church and Jane was happy to help.

The church was packed. Martin had many friends. All knew him to be an honest, conscientious and dependable man and a good friend. Margo sobbed as she read the eulogy, her heart breaking. Many of the neighboring men spoke so highly of her dad.

After the funeral was over, Cedric's mother drove Eve and Margo home, then stayed with them, making sure they took nourishment and rested. A few days passed. Eve decided to check Martin's computer and paperwork to make sure all accounts had been paid. Searching through his top drawer she discovered an envelope with 'Insurance' written on the front – opening it, she found to her surprise a life insurance policy to the amount of five hundred thousand dollars. Eve's heart raced – it was to be paid to her if he died from accidental death or of natural causes. Martin had prepared for his departure into eternity and left the women well provided for. She ran as fast as she could to the stables, calling, "Margo, Margo come and see what Martin has left for us."

They hugged each other and cried, their sad tears turning to tears of joy – Margo would be able to go to university and then go onto Business College. She would have a fine future ahead - with no money worries. They turned their faces heavenwards and both thanked their Heavenly Father in gratitude.

The Property Owner Visits Eve

*I*an Dale, the owner of the property where Martin had worked, came to visit Eve one morning - he had a special reason. He handed Eve a cheque – the amount was quite substantial.

Eve could not believe her eyes and said, before bursting into tears, "I can't accept this - you paid Martin very well – more than the regular wage. It's too much!"

Ian took Eve's hand and said, "Over the years I put a certain amount of Martin's pay into an investment fund – this cheque is yours, you can reinvest it or spend it. Please keep it and use it wherever you need to, this is a gift from your dear husband, Martin."

Ian continued. "And there's more. You also now own this house and four hectares of land." Eve was still tearful as Ian said goodbye. Taking Eve's hand he said, "Anytime you need help, give me a call."

Eve thought about Martin and his devotion to his work – he spent many hours looking after the foaling of the brood mares, sometimes staying up all night with a mare when she was giving birth and saving many foals from being trampled on or dying from suffocation.

Angela

Margo Leaves Home

University was about to commence. Margo had packed her car and was ready to leave - her new blue Mazda loaded to the hilt. She had been practicing driving it as it was automatic, unlike the only other vehicle she had driven, her dad's Land Rover. No more gear changing – so easy – her automatic car glided along so smoothly she didn't feel one bump in the gravel road. The old Land Rover belonged to Eve now; she would drive it until it clapped out.

Mother and daughter shed tears as they parted. As she leaned into her mother's shoulder, Margo knew that their wonderful neighbours would look after Eve. She had many friends, who attended the same craft classes. Sketching was by far her favourite hobby.

Margo settled quickly into university life. Her new blue Mazda impressed the other students – all wanting to have a turn at driving it, though Margo refused. There was one girl though who was often in the passenger seat. Her name was Angela Austen; she came from Hong Kong and had just started university as well. They became firm friends and spent many hours studying together in their cramped conditions - four girls renting the one house. So Margo and Angela decided that after the holidays they would search for a suitable unit to share.

Angie thoroughly enjoyed holidaying with Margo – she had her first ride on a horse and a first swim in the dam. After living in a crowded city, the property and activities were like heaven to Angie.

They returned to Brisbane determined to find a suitable unit. They had reserved a week of their holidays and hoped to settle into a unit before the next semester. They found a two-bedroom unit, with a large bathroom and kitchen/living area. The move went smoothly, both girls excited about having their own space.

Unit Living & University Life

Uni life continued on - both girls studying hard, determined to do well in their courses. Their unit was only fifteen minutes' drive from the university. They had added a few extra decorations to the unit and it looked like a very comfortable home. Now they had a place of their own, Eve could come to Brisbane and stay awhile. Margo's room was large enough to fit two single beds plus wardrobes and a large duchess. Eve enjoyed her trips to the city and decided shopping there for clothes and shoes was much cheaper.

The time passed and eventually the girls finished university, both hoping to gain high marks. They went to their respective homes for the holidays to wait for university results.

When Margo returned home, she found Eve jubilant about her sketching efforts; she was becoming well known in her district. Both women danced around, laughing happily together.

News came through via phone, Margo's university results were good – exactly what she hoped to achieve.

She phoned Angie who had also received high marks. Now both could go back to Brisbane and apply to go to Business College.

Back to Brisbane & Business College

*B*oth girls gained acceptance to Business College where they would learn how to conduct themselves when applying for a job. They would learn deportment, how to suitably dress before being interviewed, how to apply make up, and the correct words to use to impress the interviewer. After their year of studies, both girls felt well prepared to search for work the following year.

At the end of the year, they spent time with Eve on the property, both waiting for their results from the college. When they arrived, they knew their high marks would enable both of them to submit the best qualifications, and be the first ones to be interviewed.

Margo and Angie had inquired about work at many companies. The one Margo was interested in mainly was called 'Australian Textiles'. If she worked there, the opportunity to increase her knowledge would be boundless. Margo was an inquisitive person – she needed a job where she could keep on learning new skills and gain more knowledge. Her energy encouraged Angie, who would just coast along without Margo's enthusiasm.

Margo awakened to her phone ringing – she wondered if this might be one of the companies calling her now. Lifting the phone nervously, she said, "Hello."

A deep voice asked, "Are you Margo? I'm Paul, the manager of 'Australian Textiles' and I would like to interview you. Would you be available for an interview tomorrow?"

Overjoyed, Margo enthusiasticly replied, "Yes," then inquired where. Paul gave her the address. Margo could not contain her excitement – she and Angie waltzed around the room, two very excited young women.

Her next thought was, 'What will I wear?' Fossicking through the wardrobe, Margo spied a pink suit, "This will be just the right thing."

The Interview

Margo dressed carefully, giving detailed attention to her make up. Her nails had been freshly painted and the pink suit was exactly the right apparel to wear. She took a quick approving look in the mirror, then she and Angie set out early.

Angie drove the Mazda – she could find her way around to unknown areas of Brisbane. They planned a celebratory luncheon after the interview and some shopping for suitable clothes for an office working girl.

The interview went well, conducted by Paul, who introduced himself as Chief Executive of the company. He was courteous and pleasant and Margo's nervousness abated. She felt rather composed and was able to answer all Paul's questions without a falter in her voice.

*   *   *   *   *

Angie could not contain her inquisitiveness and anxiously asked, "Well, what was he like – did the interview go well?"

Margo said, "I think so Angie. He was such an amicable man I immediately felt at ease after meeting him and I relaxed".

After the day's activities they returned to their unit, exhausted and excited.

Margo Works at Australian Textiles

*T*he phone call came the following day. Both Margo and Angie drove into town to become familiar with the office. Margo was taking over the office of a staff member who was leaving very soon to be married. A woman named Cherie was in charge of orientating the office staff and took Margo to where her office was situated.

Sitting in her plush chair, Margo felt so very comfortable. She was sure she would enjoy working there after being shown the type of work that she had to do.

Angie became engrossed in conversation with Cherie and inquired if there might be another position for her later on. After perusing Angie's business credentials, which she had brought along just in case, Cherie suggested that she have an interview with the chief.

Angie replied, "I'm not really suitably dressed today."

Cherie rang Paul, then hurried her to his office saying, "Paul's available now."

Angie's interview went well. Another staff member was leaving next month – she hoped to travel and see Europe, Angie could take her place. The Chief Executive was equally impressed with Angie's reports and her personality, and she was accepted as well.

Both of them were exuberantly happy – they danced around their living room, and then each said a prayer of thanks to the Lord for His provisions into the type of work they were trained to do.

They would start work the following week. While they waited to commence work they shopped for suitable clothes to wear to work - a colourful blouse under a dull suit! Eve was excited for the girls, especially with both working for the same company.

Employment

*T*he office was buzzing with excited giggling and chattering. John Trelor, the owner of 'Australian Textiles,' was holding a Christmas party and everyone had received an invitation – including the cleaners and the young man who delivered office essentials. No one was left out. This was great news. Margo had thought of taking her mum, Eve, overseas – they would visit Hong Kong and spend a few days with Angie's family – but that would be put on hold for now anyway.

Usually John worked in his laboratory, which was in a building set apart from the main office. When he occasionally walked through the office area Margo's heart

John

missed a beat – he had a certain aura about him.

Angie was a party person. She'd noticed a certain guy who had delivered office essentials – she hoped to meet up with him at the party, which was to be celebrated at John's home.

There was plenty of time to shop for party clothes. The girls took their time to choose because it would be a glamorous affair. Angie chose a short blue dress and matching accessories. Margo took much longer, she found it hard to decide and in the end Angie chose for her, a three quarter length emerald green gown. Margo tried it on and they both caught their breath - the dress fitted perfectly and, with her auburn hair, she created a stunning picture in the mirror.

Margo Meets John at the Christmas Party

As Margo and Angie arrived at John's home, all heads turned, but one man in particular noticed their entrance. Angie went for drinks and Margo was left alone – she felt at a loss as there she stood. She was in her late twenties and had never been to such a classy party.

She was about to return through the entrance doorway, when a voice said, "I haven't had the pleasure of meeting you. My name's John." He held out his hand.

Margo turned around. She knew that voice - it was the owner, John. Momentarily tongue-tied, she replied in a tiny voice, "I'm Margo." Their eyes met in recognition of each other.

Angie arrived with the drinks and all three conversed for a short time, then Angie spotted her 'dream boat' and left to pursue him.

The party finished late. Margo and John were so engrossed in their conversation that they forgot how much time had passed. Finally someone called, "Speech, John." He looked at his watch – it was past midnight.

"Thank you for coming to my party. Thank you for all your hard work and for working long hours, also for your loyalty to my company and me. Thank you for keeping it running smoothly."

John finished off by saying, "Merry Christmas to you all and may God bless each and everyone here – remember Jesus is the reason for the season. Have a safe and enjoyable holiday."

He came over to Margo and Angie, kissed them both on the cheek, then said to Margo, "I would like to take you to dinner one evening soon. I'll see you at the office on Monday." Margo's heart leapt, but she tried not to let her eyes betray her feelings.

Party Over

It was Saturday – the rain pelted down. The women slept in. Angie made tea and toast for their breakfast and took it into Margo's room; she was intrigued about John and Margo's chat. Margo didn't say much except that John was very easy to talk to, and she really enjoyed his company. Both agreed that John's palatial home would be lovely to live in and his choice of party food was scrumptious. Angie could tell that Margo was more than interested in John, and she was over the moon for her.

John could not forget the woman in the emerald dress - why had he not noticed her before? Her beautiful auburn hair glowed in the softness of the Christmas fairy lights. He must see more of this woman and he would take her to dinner soon.

*   *   *   *   *

Margo and John often dined out – six weeks had passed since the party and John decided he must propose to Margo, he didn't want to let her escape - they were the perfect couple.

A few days after Margo accepted John's proposal, he decided to take his sons Enrich and Stephan out to dine with himself and his lovely fiancé. He announced their engagement, placing the one-carat diamond ring on Margo's finger. She was overwhelmed and it showed, but also a little unsettled as his sons did not congratulate them and excused themselves soon after the meal was over.

John held her hand and explained to her about his first wife's death when the boys were young. He and his wife had married before they were twenty and the boys had been born in the next two years. His wife had died from cancer when the boys were five and six years old. In the following years they had become a very close-knit family – they would need time to adjust to their dad's new fiancé.

Uniforms And Work

Margo was anxious to see where John worked in the laboratory, where he experimented with different types of thread such as wool, cotton and synthetics. He had wanted to produce a cloth for men's suits that would be permanent press and a non-stretch fabric that would not shine or seat. He had succeeded in producing this cloth and was overjoyed to show Margo.

While congratulating John, Margo suggested producing a cloth that would be useful to make women's suits; perhaps a suit that could be worn as their office uniform. John was interested and delighted that Margo wanted to be involved in the company. They decided to add more colour to the fabric. Margo said, "I'll design a uniform and ask the others in the office to give their opinions."

The office staff was excited about having a special uniform with the 'Australian Textiles' insignia on the jacket. There were many others who would like to work there, they had heard of the splendid office, and the pay packet was not to be blinked at.

Church – Margo's Story

John, Angie and I usually attended St Paul's church together. Today I went alone – John was in Paris with his son Enrich and Angie had gone home to Hong Kong, as her mother had been taken ill and was in hospital.

The service was good; the middle-aged pastor gave a wonderful sermon about Jesus' birth. He was most descriptive of that special night.

He said, "As Christmas draws near, that wonderful event of Jesus' birth over two thousand years ago comes to mind. I imagine the glorious singing of the angels as they welcomed Jesus into this world – what a special event it was. What joy comes to our minds and hearts when we remember why He came. Such jubilant celebrations echoed across the hills and the valleys – a special child sent to us in a special way by God his Father, to bring forgiveness and to show His love to all mankind.

It was a beautiful moonlit night - a quietness - a hush! Settled over the hills and the valleys, an aura of expectancy surrounds all who are awaiting Jesus' birth.

The atmosphere is like a controlled excitement – Joyful yet peaceful, as though all creation is waiting! Waiting! Can you picture all this in your minds? The air becomes filled with the sound of music as the angelic choir and Heavenly throng burst forth in praise of this blessed event."

The pastor's descriptions of Jesus' birth filled me with ecstatic joy, his preaching gave me a new insight into that event as I walked down to the building at the back of the church yard where I usually give the flowers clean water to keep them fresh for the evening service.

I was not prepared for the next event in my life.

Locked In

I carried the flowers down the six steps into the brick building and started to empty the water. Suddenly there was a loud bang and I jumped with shock. The door had slammed closed, but there wasn't even a breeze blowing. I walked up the stairs and tugged on the door, it was shut fast, and it would not budge. I tried again - it was closed and locked. The key was on the outside; I always left it there.

I said out loud, "What will I do?" I rummaged in my handbag, "My phone's not here, I must have left it at home on the table. Anyway, there's no one to ring - Angie's in Hong Kong and John is in Paris".

I had to confront reality – someone had locked me in. I sat on the chair bewildered, wondering who would do such a thing? I had no enemies. I tried calling out, which was useless – this was a double brick walled room. I looked up at the high windows, 'No way of escape through those,' I thought, and then decided to look around.

There were two large towels. I also found tea, coffee and chicken noodle soup in the cupboards, a metho stove and a bottle of methylated spirits. 'Someone used to live here a long time ago by the date on the soup packets,' I thought.

Night time came. I placed the towels on the floor and sat there, leaning my back against the cold brick wall, 'Looks like I'll have to bed down here tonight.' Luckily I had worn a warm suit and stockings.

I woke early - someone opened the door and placed a plate of food on the step. I called out as I scrambled to my feet, "Let me out of here! Why are you doing this?"

The door closed quickly, and I heard the key turn in the lock. I called out again, and then heard the purring of a car engine driving away.

I picked up the plate of food. I was hungry; I hadn't eaten since Sunday breakfast. Then I thought, 'I won't eat this - it may be poisoned. If whoever locked me in here doesn't like me, he or she may try to feed me poisoned food,' so I threw it in the bin.

The Dungeon

I thought of the apostle Paul and of Peter when they were locked in dungeons, and began to call this room my dungeon.

It was dark and dismal in the dungeon, however there was an electric light that I switched on to read my bible. I prayed, ' God, please help me escape!' Every hour or two I prayed this *prayer and read the Psalms, where I read, 'My help comes from the Lord who made Heaven and earth,' and I knew my Heavenly Father would help me devise a way of escape. I knew I should focus on the positives, but it was hard not knowing what would happen next.*

I made myself a cup of tea and tried the chicken noodle soup. 'It tastes all right, I guess.' Hunger helped me not to notice its staleness, and the hot mixtures helped me warm up.

Night came around again. I wrote in my diary, keeping track of time, day and date – if anyone found me one day, all that was happening to me was recorded. I slept intermittently and talked to my Heavenly Father as though He was right beside me.

I had been rejected by Cedric, which took me a long time to recover from. However I had studied hard and engrossed myself in my studies to block all thoughts of my first love out. Cedric had travelled overseas and I didn't see him again which was a blessing in disguise - out of sight, out of mind - and I had eventually stopped thinking about him. Then I had met John.

I reminisced, mainly thinking about my engagement to John. I had taken him to Eve's property and he enjoyed the weekend there. We went riding and Eve and John 'hit it off', as they say. Mum was thrilled by my choice. John enjoyed the horse ride and all the property had to offer.

I remembered what John had told me about Blanch, his first wife. They had married when they were both nearly twenty years old. She was a tiny lady who loved to shop, spending dollars on clothes, handbags, shoes and lingerie – she always looked beautiful. If they spent the night at home, he, John, cooked the dinner while Blanch read stories to Enrich and Stephan after she put them to bed – they were very happy. John had said he didn't mind her outrageous spending as he had plenty for her to spend frivolously and he absolutely adored her. When she passed away, the boys fretted and he fretted also, though her presence with them was still very strong for a very long time. She had the sweetest nature and John had never met anyone like her.

John Searches for Margo

John arrived back from Paris very early on Monday and went to see Margo as soon as he left the airport. Her unit looked deserted, the blinds were drawn. He called her number again, no answer, then he called Angie. She was on her way home and didn't have a clue where Margo would have gone.

Eve phoned John, she was worried, she could not raise Margo on the phone. When John asked when she had last heard from Margo, she replied, "On Sunday morning before she left for church. I'm flying to Brisbane, John."

It was after John's call from Eve that he called the police, who put up posters and photos of Margo. John did not waste any time, he even spoke to a private investigator, who began to search for Margo also. She had been missing since Sunday and it was now Wednesday afternoon.

Escape – Margo's Story

As I prayed one morning, a plan started to form in my mind - I must try to escape before I become too weak. Still too afraid of being poisoned, I didn't eat the food that was deposited every day.

I decided to stand behind the door on the landing at the top step and when I saw the door start to open inwards I would pull it very hard. I wasn't sure if this idea would work but I had to try.

Today was Friday - this might be my last chance to try to escape as I was starting to feel very weak. I heard a motorcar ever so quietly pull up, so I was ready. As the door opened and a hand appeared with food, I tugged the door with all my energy and a figure came tumbling down the steps. I crawled out, pulling the door shut behind me and turning the key. I looked around for my car which I'd parked in the church parking lot last Sunday morning, but it had disappeared. As I was feeling faint, I went then and sat in the car that my captor had arrived in.

When I recovered slightly I saw a phone on the adjoining seat. I dialed 000 then passed out. As I came to, a voice was calling, "Where are you?"

I said weakly, " I am behind St Andrews church in the dungeon,"

The voice said, "Where?"

"*In Palmer Street. Come quickly!*"

I felt safe now and started to relax, quoting, 'My help cometh from the Lord'. And then I fainted again.

An ambulance and a police van arrived. I awoke to a policeman shaking my shoulder, "Who are you? What is your name?"

I said, "Margo," then the officer phoned John, who had been searching for days and had the police involved.

The ambulance officer checked me, and then John arrived. He could not believe his eyes when he saw me – I looked pitiful.

He held me in his arms and said, "My lovely Margo, what has happened to you? Who has done this to you? "

I knew John was with me, God had answered my prayers - I was free. Again I fainted.

Margo in Hospital

Eve and Angie arrived at the hospital. Margo had been sedated, and she looked peaceful. The women and John kept an all-night vigil. Margo slept right through until Saturday afternoon.

Meanwhile the police found Margo's handbag she'd dropped on the lawn during her escape. While searching through it, an officer found her diary. He looked through it and read from the date she disappeared until today. She had written about being locked in a dungeon, about throwing out the suspected poisoned food and her plan to escape.

The second policeman searched further and noticed the key in the door of the brick building - he called the other officer over. When they unlocked and opened the door, the men could not believe what they saw - a man lying on the floor in a pool of blood. The older policeman said, "This looks like a case for the boss. You stay on guard, I'll go and fetch reinforcements."

Stephan In Hospital

The police phoned John. They had found his son Stephan in a critical condition with a broken neck and a head wound. He had been admitted to the same hospital as Margo. The doctor confirmed Stephan's condition and told John where he was found. He was puzzled by the circumstances when the police explained how they had found Margo in Stephan's car and that she had used his phone to dial 000 for help.

Margo explained to them that she had been locked up in a 'dungeon' and pointed to the room behind St Luke's Church. This was where his son was found badly injured. John mused, 'What connection would my son and fiancé have?' He was completely overwhelmed by the whole episode.

Eve stayed by Margo's hospital bed as she continued to improve. She received the best care, however a very real fear of the unknown still haunted her. Eve knew how frightened her daughter was, but neither woman knew that Stephan was the culprit, the person who had incarcerated Margo, and neither knew that he had been admitted to the same hospital.

John told Margo about his son being found in such a critical state. He knew there must be some connection but his mind could not unravel the puzzle. This piece of information upset Margo, who decided she must run away - she must not cause John's family to break up.

Eventually Margo was well enough to leave the hospital and John insisted that she come to his place to recuperate. He would employ a nurse and a housekeeper to take care of her.

John & Margo's Special Dinner

Margo's next few days appeared much happier - she would keep up the facade to please John. He had invited her out to dinner at the "Palatial Restaurant" and asked Margo to wear her emerald green dress. Margo thanked God for knowing this wonderful man, but she knew by now that John's son, Stephan, despised her. She decided she must leave tomorrow - she would not take responsibility for parting John from his family.

It was a beautiful night, a bright moon shone, the two lovers focusing only on each other. Margo's laughter cheered John - she pretended she was happy although under her happy facade her heart was sad. Margo kept her anxiety and all her sad emotions under control and immersed herself in this wonderful evening with John. The dinner went well, Margo wished it would never end, and John said, "We must set a wedding date soon." As their dinner date ended John said, "We must bring this enjoyable evening to a close, time to return home. I have to pack, the plane to Paris leaves early tomorrow."

Margo was very tired so she changed quickly and went to bed - sadness was starting to encompass her. John followed and, as always, lay beside her and talked until she fell asleep, then he walked into the adjoining bedroom to sleep.

Two Women Missing

Meanwhile Angie devised a plan of escape - she and Margo would disappear. She knew that Margo was in a delicate condition and if they both went away Margo would be able to settle down and focus on the positives. To stay would mean having to face court cases and confront reality - she was in too much of a dilemma to face any more police questioning.

Angie knew much of the whole story now that John had told Eve and her about his son being involved. Being most resourceful, she would plan a secret escape. Each day she visited Margo, carrying with her a brief case and an overnight bag. She always washed Margo's clothes and returned clean clothes. She and Margo discussed the plan though Margo was hesitant to leave John. But she knew that she had to get away, far away, especially when John told her about Stephan's critical condition and where he had been found. Margo realised that John's loyalty was to his family, and her jailor was John's son.

Angie's plan was in place. She managed to get the insurance from Margo's stolen car, as the car had not been found after its disappearance from the church car park. She also gave away most of their belongings, even travelling out of Brisbane for a few days to swap her car for a larger one.

Now that Margo felt a lot stronger the friends had been lunching and shopping daily. So the day they left saying,

"We are off to the shops and to have lunch down town," no one batted an eyelid, no one asked any questions.

Angie and Margo had gradually withdrawn all monies from their bank accounts, a few hundred dollars each time, until all accounts were depleted. The women were on their way and travelling west. Anyone who discovered they were missing would probably either travel north or south to find them. They deliberately chose to leave while John spent time overseas, in Paris.

Runaway Women

After travelling into Toowoomba the women decided to have their hair cut and tinted. Margo shed tears as her lovely auburn locks fell to the floor in a heap, with the hairdresser comforting her. It was her first haircut for many years – her hair was her pride and joy, now most of it was gone. Margo's hair was tinted black and Angie chose blonde.

Visiting different boutiques helped them discover the type of clothes they had not worn before. They found the platform shoes hard to walk in and the large brimmed hats hard to keep on, as it was a windy day. The long scarfs and loose flowery blouses flapped around their bodies. But they were new women now and would change their names as well.

They stopped at the next town for the night, choosing to chalk up as many kilometres from Brisbane as they could on their first few days. Margo was now more dependent on her friend, Angie. She knew that underneath Angie's frivolous facade there was a strong, determined, loyal personality - Angie made things happen.

They were a little cautious too, knowing that hidden in the car were hundreds of dollars, most of it hidden in the lining of their handbags and backpacks. The women travelled on towards Lightning Ridge, deciding to explore the opal miners' homes, churches and hotels and to experience sleeping underground, savouring the food and experiencing how the other half lived, before heading north to Charlieville.

The women looked nothing like the friends from Brisbane - no one would recognise them. However, they did not always stay together, often spending the night in separate hotels or motels.

Their plan was to crisscross the countryside, not going in any one direction, so if anyone tried to follow their trail it would be hard going. That way both women would not be easily identifiable.

Westward Ho

Angie and Margo were intrigued, wondering how anyone ever lived in these outback wayward places and conditions. Petrol as well as food became more expensive but they had done their homework before leaving Brisbane. They knew that freight costs caused the higher western prices, which they were prepared for. At last they reached Longreach

- the dusty roads worsened and the corrugations shook them up. They were always ready to shower every night.

Today they would spend time in the 'Hall of Fame' they had heard so much about. They found it very interesting and spent hours and hours there. The memorabilia had been collected over many years - it was all Australian history. Those who collated it were truly dedicated to the work. After visiting the 'Hall of Fame' they decided that jeans and check shirts should be their dress now as most people outback wore casual clothes.

Their new names were Francis and Dora and they would decide on a surname when they settled somewhere.

After visiting and exploring many outback towns, the women drove south, deciding to drive the Great Ocean Road which was a long way further south in Victoria. They drove through so many country towns on the way, only remembering a few of the names until they reached Shepparton.

John Searches Everywhere

*J*ohn arrived back from Paris – his venture overseas was to his son Enrich's office, as there had been a few hiccups he had to sort out. Stephan was continuing to improve. He would be crippled and would not be able to work, his head injuries had been critical. The medical team was surprised at how fast his recovery was progressing - he had a strong determination.

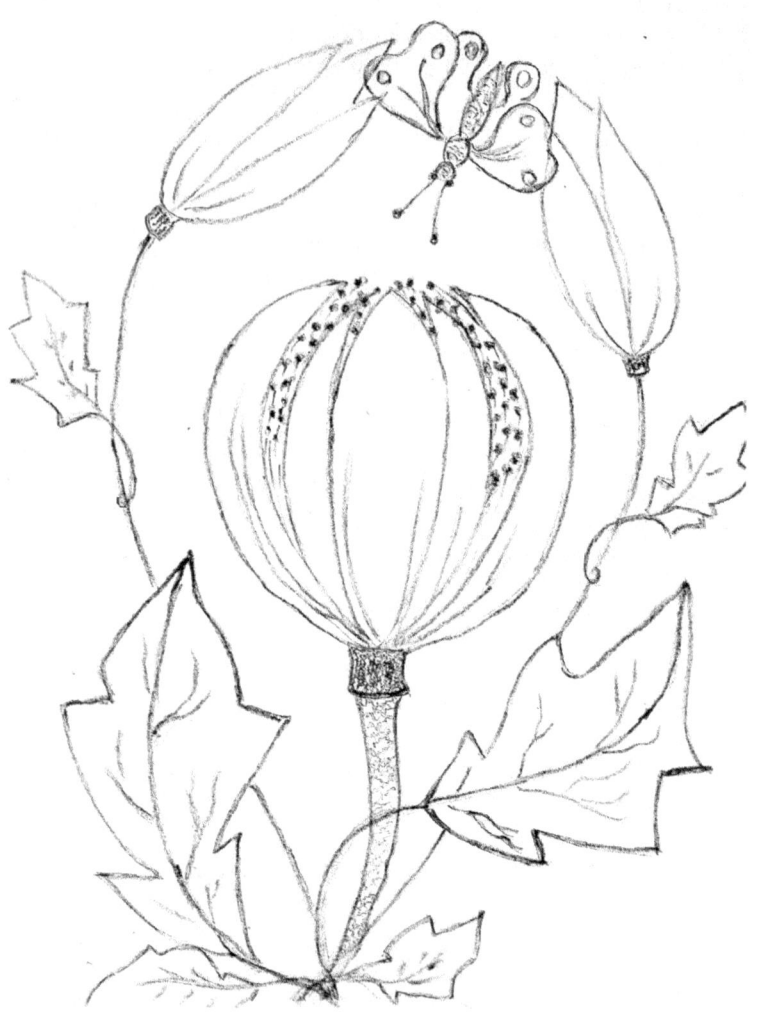

Margo had phoned John before he left Paris and she seemed more at ease, more contented – 'no worries there', he thought. He was a happy man knowing they would marry soon. When he arrived back in Brisbane he went straight to Margo's unit, noticing all the blinds were drawn. He knocked on the door. No answer. 'Oh well', he thought, Margo must have driven over to Eve's for a few days as she was still on sick leave.

He arrived at the office and asked Cherie if she had heard from either Margo or Angie. Cherie replied that she had not. Now John began to worry. 'Has she disappeared again?' he thought, 'I will phone Eve, they both may be there.'

"They called in," said Eve, "said they intended to travel around to see a few places they had not been to before the holidays ended."

This was a dilemma to John - Margo didn't mention travel when she phoned him last time, and he did not expect silence from his new love.

John's Search Begins

A week had transpired since John arrived back from overseas. He felt he had to do something so he discussed Margo's disappearance with the police. They also were interested in Margo, the whole truth about her missing previously still needed sorting out.

John knew why Margo had been incarcerated; his son Stephan was the culprit who had jailed her. His jealousy had caused him to take revenge. John could not understand such thinking and actions by his son. Stephan's jealousy had blinded him and now the repercussions of his appalling act would be all over the newspapers if John did not take action. He pleaded with the police not to take Stephan into custody – he had suffered enough, and would they please close the case.

John heard no more from the police and now he decided to employ a private investigator he knew, a very good one, who would help him track down the missing women. Les Mulligan was a good friend and if it took him ten years, he would keep on the case.

Descriptions of the women, their style of dress, car number plates - Les had the lot though little did he know all had changed. The girl's secrecy disturbed both men - the closed bank accounts and the suddenness of their departure challenged both men to find them, no matter how long or how widely the search continued on.

On a hunch, Les travelled north west to Toowoomba, where there were many Hair Salons. He knew from past experience that the women would probably colour their hair and choose a new hairstyle. One young hairdresser he spoke to said that she actually cut Margo's long auburn hair and remembered how Margo cried as she said she had not had her hair cut before. And yes, the shorter woman chose to blond her hair. The shorter one had also asked about the 'Outback', what was it like? The hairdresser had told them it was hot and dusty.

Les drove to Goondiwindi, hoping he was on their trail. There he asked a few questions around the town – choosing cafes and motels. Yes, his enquiries gave him positive answers, however the women did not appear to be like the picture on the posters, though the difference in their heights matched. People also confirmed that they drove further west. Les gathered that the women were zigzagging around so as to confuse anyone who might be on their trail.

Every night Les would play the video of Margo and Angie laughing together in happier times, this helped him to remember them. He noticed how they walked and talked and their actions, any small idiosyncrasies which would help him recognise them. Les had a strong memory for faces and voices which always helped him in his quest to find the escapees or missing persons. He kept on doggedly pursuing every avenue possible.

Les drove from Goondiwindi across to Mungindi thinking, if there were any positive leads there, he would drive on to Lightning Ridge. Les' hunch was correct, the women had stayed at Lightning Ridge for a few days and seemed to enjoy sleeping underground in the dug-out homes. They had even tried their luck at 'noodling' for opals before moving on again.

Les knew he was on the right trail. He imagined they would keep going north now. At each town he was proved right because there was talk of these two women who were dressed in completely the wrong clothes for the outback - they wore flowing blouses, trousers, scarves and floppy hats – not jeans like everyone else.

After visiting and enquiring at towns such as St George and Roma, Les travelled on to Charleville and surmised the women would visit Longreach to see the Hall of Fame. He was right again, however after leaving there he was not sure which way to go, but suspected they would back track now. This took him many weeks. The women had been noticed when they returned to some of the places and it appeared that they were now southward bound.

After travelling to Bourke then onto Nyngan, Dubbo and Orange, he lost their trail. The young women had definitely gone south, then probably to Melbourne. Les could find no leads in Melbourne and headed back home, frustrated. Back in Brisbane, Les went to see John who agreed with him that the women would most likely keep travelling and would finally settle in Melbourne.

Les decided he would take some time off work, he knew he was confident of picking up their trail later.

On The Road

After travelling for nearly two months the women were becoming weary of it all and wanted to find a place to settle for good. They decided to travel further south to Melbourne, this would take a few more weeks. Once they decided where they wanted to go their spirits lifted. They prayed for guidance and turned towards the south. Although Margo phoned Eve and kept in touch, Eve had no idea where she phoned from and pretended to John that she had not heard any more from the women.

The young women travelled through many more towns, stopping overnight in separate motels. To keep their focus on why they were running away, they must not let their guard down.

After arriving at the outskirts of Melbourne very late one afternoon, they were driving into an outer suburb that looked so beautiful with lovely trees growing on both sides of a side street. They decided to stop there. Tired out, both women booked into the same room. Money was running low and they needed to settle and to find some kind of employment.

Both decided to work cleaning motels or hotels until they could find the kind of work they were trained to do. They decided to go to a fitness centre where they would gain information about work that was available in Melbourne from notices pinned to the bulletin board. They also read the jobs columns in the newspapers.

Melbourne

Still maintaining their caution, the next day they were separately interviewed by estate agents, each wanting a unit of their own, quickly finding suitable units not too far from each other. Without Angie, Margo felt lost and alone, abandoned. This feeling stemmed from her being locked up in the room near the church. She longed to return to the normal Margo once she returned to work and settled into city life. Margo needed to travel by public transport and would buy a second hand car when she had a paying job.

Giving their names as Dora Lane and Francie Fielding as they were introduced around, they were amused one day when they were introduced to each other by a girl called Ruby.

After gathering the information needed, the women

decided to have their names legally changed before both decided to train at a TAFE college to become kindergarten teachers. Margo (Dora) was happy - she loved children. However, Angie (Fran) found there was an opening for shop and office cleaners - she was more interested in that. That night they met for dinner and discussed their futures. Both were happy with Fran's idea that she would work from 3am to 8am and then be free to sleep and shop most days. As Fran loved to shop, this would be an ideal job for her.

One day Fran said to Dora with a laugh, "I think we should take elocution lessons. Did you notice the locals' accents? They speak as though they have plums in their mouths."

Dora had noticed the difference. Queenslanders' have a slower way of speaking and, the further south one travels, people speak much faster and sound more refined. They were asked sometimes if they were Texans, so elocution lessons they must have. They were quick to learn because working alongside other Melbournians helped them to practice their new accents.

Paying cash so that it would be harder for someone to trace their calls, they bought new mobile phones. By now they were believing that John would have given up trying to find them, so they moved into a shared unit and Dora decorated it, both feeling calmer and safer now. Because of their new names, new phones, different dress and speech, they were different people. They had opened up banking accounts in their new names and believed they were now safe from being identified

Close by they found a church with a youngish pastor. He was pleased to have younger women in his congregation as most who went to his church were sixty and older. The women surmised his age to be fortyish. He introduced himself as Timothy Blair. Fran and Dora, when introducing themselves, nearly tripped up about their new names but Tim did not appear to notice.

Over the weeks the three became firm friends and Tim invited them to the parsonage for a meal. The women accepted and found Tim was a great cook. He had lived alone for ten years and knew how to bake a dinner. Tim was invited to their unit at weekends to play table games, all enjoying one another's company.

When the cold winter turned to spring, Tim invited them to go to Ocean Reef beach after the service on Sundays. There was a shop there that sold light refreshments, however Tim always packed his hamper and Dora often made a slice or a cake to take.

Ocean Reef Outings

Over two years had passed since Dora and Fran had left Brisbane. While on a Sunday picnic at Ocean Reef beach, Fran noticed a man sitting on a seat close by, reading a newspaper. Every now and then he would look over and, when Fran looked back at him, he turned away. This happened each time they were there. Next time without hesitation Fran called him over and said, "Thought you looked lonely, come and enjoy a coffee with us."

He introduced himself as Les Mulligan, said he was alone, hoped to catch a sea breeze. He was a photographer - it

was his hobby. He was paid by magazines to take shots of people near the sea or swimming. Straight away he took a photo of them all. After Les left, Dora picked up the paper Les left there - it was a Queensland paper from Brisbane. Dora become agitated and said to Fran, "I wonder if John is searching for us?" Both pondered over this and stopped visiting Ocean Reef beach, making excuses that Tim found puzzling.

After a few weeks the weather heated up and they went back with Tim to their favourite seaside beach. The coast was clear. With no sign of Les, both girls relaxed.

However the following Sunday the photographer was back. He looked at them through binoculars. Tim had also a set of binoculars and looked over at Les. There was also another man with Les, and they were both looking towards them.

John Finds His True Love

*T*wo weeks later the trio went back to their favourite beach. The women could not see the men and felt that their imaginations had been playing games with them and so they relaxed, enjoying the lunches from the Snack Shack. They packed up and went for a leisurely walk along the wharf, stopping for a while leaning over the wharf rail, drinking in the cool salty air and watching the sea.

A voice startled Dora. A man walked over to her and said, "I hoped you might like some company."

Dora was horrified until recognition dawned on her - it

was her John! She ran into his outstretched arms without hesitation saying, "You have found me!" They hugged and kissed and cried, laughing mostly, full of happiness, their love had stood the test of time.

John's private investigator, Les, was the cameraman. Today they had been there hiding amongst the trees, so John could try to work out if it was really his Margo.

Tim looked bewildered, why did this man call Dora 'Margo'? Who were these women he thought he knew?

Les grinned from ear to ear, "Another success story," he said out loud as he walked away.

John called Les back and said, "Les has kept me from giving up. Would you all mind if we bow our heads and give thanks to God?"

Tim was completely in awe of what had just happened and stood transfixed to the spot.

The Story Revealed To Pastor Tim

"Don't let Margo out of your sight again, John," said Les as he said goodbye to them all, thanking Dora and Fran for the hospitality they had shown him.

John explained that he nearly gave up the search - it was Les who kept giving him encouragement to keep looking, despite having lost their trail. Les had eventually found their legal change of name and traced them from there. Tim was introduced to John and they left the beach. After arriving back at the women's unit, Dora said to Tim, "We need to explain and apologise to you, Tim."

"Yes, you are cool customers - I never doubted who you said you were. I thought I was a most discerning person. Instead of two women named Fran and Dora, you are two female fugitives named Margo and Angie - running away from the law!" said Tim, shaking his head every now and then as he listened to their story. He was flabbergasted!

The next day Dora phoned into work to say that a family crisis had arisen so she would not be in. Fran went to work then did some shopping, knowing it best to leave John and Margo alone – they had a lot to discuss. John had many questions, although he was beginning to understand that Margo had not wanted to break up his family. "Stephan committed suicide," he told Margo. "His life was ruined - he was a cripple. A car accident would finish his life – those were Stephan's final thoughts."

Dora And Margo

Margo would always be Margo to John, so she legally reversed her name change to please John, and Eve her mother. Her auburn hair would grow back. John stayed with Margo and Fran for a week, he and Margo discussing their future together. To concentrate all her time on John, Margo went back to work and gave notice. As John watched her with the kindergarten children and how they responded to her, a smile crossed his face. He hoped he and Margo would have children together.

Eve decided to move to Melbourne and live with Margo

until after the wedding. John would move the textile business to Paris as Enrich had married happily and was living permanently there. He also decided to buy Eve's property – he and Margo would spend some of their holidays there, taking Eve with them.

The wedding had to be planned. Pastor Tim would marry John and Margo, Fran would be Maid of Honour, while Enrich would be his dad's Best Man. Enrich and his bride would return to Australia and stay for a few weeks - he wanted to reunite the family that had been torn apart by his brother's stupid jealousy.

Tim and Fran

*O*bserving how Tim constantly stood at Fran's side, Margo suggested her friend give Tim a little encouragement. A romance began to develop between them. Fran cared deeply for Tim and soon they were an item, laughing and joking together often and now holding hands. 'There will be another wedding soon,' Margo thought.

Pastor Tim married John and Margo in his church. 'Angie – Fran' was the maid of honour and John's son Enrich was his dad's best man. It was so very evident to all that Enrich's wife, Veronike, was head over heels in love with him.

John and Margo decided to honeymoon at Apollo Bay. When they returned the couple found a lovely old home near the seaside, with a pleasant view. Margo was thrilled with it and to be together at last - and forever, she hoped.

Pastor Tim and Fran kept in touch with their married friends and announced their engagement at a morning church service, where all enjoyed a morning tea. Fran was overjoyed and Tim ecstatic. He had waited a long time for this exciting woman to enter his life.

Margo's Epilogue

I enjoy watching my little girls, Grace and Joy, playing on the lawn under the garden sprinklers. It's a very hot day – stifling in fact, one of those very hot dry Melbourne heat waves – it flows over me like a furnace.

It was a day much like today when John passed away. I will never forget the sadness. He had so much more living to do with Grace and Joy, however God had other plans.

It's just a year since John's departure into another place, a better place – where he's free from pain, and for this I'm thankful. We both loved the same God, the God who sent His only son to give His life a ransom, on whom many would believe, and come to repentance.

I smile as I see our little girls so happy and healthy playing on the lawn. I'll continue living in Melbourne – this is where happiness began with John – happiness that had eluded me for so long. We had fifteen years together. We were so very happy, the past was forgotten, a new future together had begun.

I've had to create another future, without John. The girls and I are happy together; we're well provided for, money is not an issue. Both girls were left a share in Australian Textiles and I have a half share, so while the business flourishes we're able to live comfortably.

John's youngest son Enrich is in control of the business and all exports. He continues experimenting with textiles and the whole business was moved to France, where Enrich, happily married, continues the business his father John began in Australia. John was so proud of his son Enrich, he knew his business was in reliable hands.

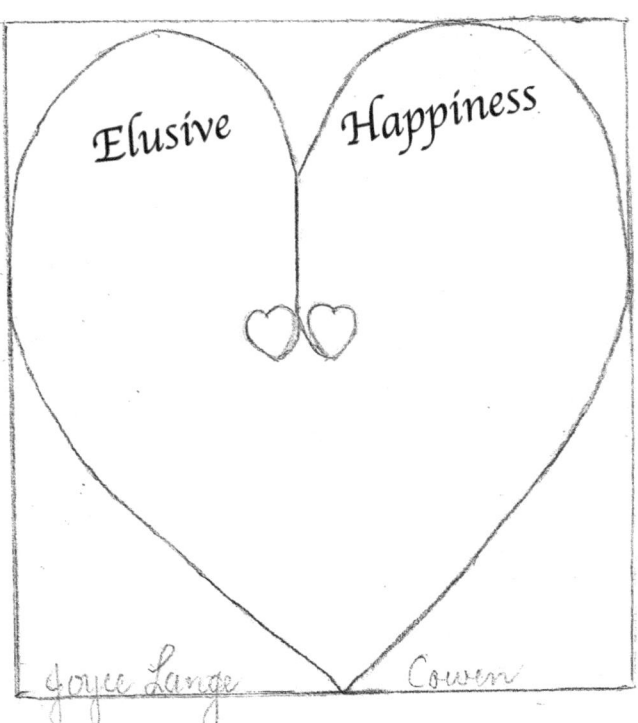